GUSTAV THEODOR FECHNER

Life After Death

I0460660

Introduction by William James

Prefatory Note by John Erskine

WILDSIDE PRESS

CONTENTS

PREFATORY NOTE

Whapter HEN the Little Book of Life After Death was published in 1836, it made an impression which a century or more has not removed. The American edition of 1904, with the introduction by William James, is here reprinted. In spite of changes and shifts in philosophy and psychology during a hundred and nine busy years, these pages still make their appeal, perhaps more than ever at this time. To some readers the appeal will lie in what is said of death. To me the lasting value of the book is in what it says of life.

Gustav Theodor Fechner was, as William James reminds us, a large figure in his day, an investigator in many fields. Most of us, no matter where our interests lie, have probably encountered one or two of his masterful ideas, or ideas inspired by him. In music I heard a reference long ago to a law which he discovered, or thought he discovered, explaining the constant relation of the physical world outside of us

7

to the physical world within. He thought that to increase an inner sensation arithmetically, the external stimulus must increase geometrically. I applied the doctrine in a region where I was somewhat at home, to the phenomenon with which musicians are familiar, that by adding to the size of an orchestra you get what may be described as a diminishing return. Though the players and their instruments each produce an equal volume of sound, two violins will not be twice as loud as one, nor will a third add as much proportionately as the second. According to Fechner's law, to make four violins sound as loud as eight, you must have sixteen. I believe psychologists have long ago disqualified this formula, but whatever the precise ratios may be, the phenomenon remains. Few musicians could make an accurate guess at the size of an orchestra if they heard it without seeing it. The eye tricks the ear. We are more than willing to believe we hear as many players as we see on the platform.

Fechner did not frame this particular law for the benefit of musicians, and the application which I made of the principle may seem remote from his discussion of life after death, but like other great psychologists, like William James himself, his hold on posterity is accounted for less by his specific contributions to psychological science than by his broadly human service in opening our eyes to the depths and the heights of our mortal days. In the Little Book of Life After Death he is in some respects, one might say, a child of Spinoza, in other respects a disciple of Plato, but he was original in observing for himself the plain truths he spreads before us, original also in the vigor with which he states those truths.

Immortality he considers a fact because it can be examined here in this present existence. Obviously he is not giving to the word the childish and too-common definition which makes of immortality merely an infinite extension of time—infinite in a queer way, since it starts only when we die. Immortality, Fechner thinks, is more than permanent duration in another world; it is a quality of life. Here and now we may choose between living a temporary life or an immortal one. Some occupations, no matter how long continued, will remain insignificant and temporary; some actions or attitudes, though we rise to them only once, are immortal.

It follows that the quality of the life we lead here determines the quality of our life after death. Fechner is not thinking of those obvious choices between goodness and wickedness which logically are rewarded or punished by heaven or by hell. He is telling us that even though we do nothing wicked, we may neglect to do anything immortal, and therefore our future prospects are as trivial as our performance now or in the past. We shall deserve to be forgotten, and the deservedly unremembered miss immortality both now and hereafter.

What assurance have we that the dead, even though they deserve immortality, will enjoy it? Fechner would have us find the answer in the experience of those who died long since, yet live in us whether or not we are conscious of them. We are born to share in the immortality of great men. But here once more Fechner makes of immortality a moral problem. No doubt the influence of saints and prophets, of our own loved ones, persists for our benefit even though we are thoughtless, but this influence comes to life, it grows and spreads when we consciously remember the good and great at their best and greatest. What sort of immortality could we look forward to, in what kind of heaven would we feel at home, if here we were careless of the noble spirits who prepared for this life of ours possibilities of wider scope and more exalted dedication?

Fechner's little book is a sermon, if you choose, but of the kind that men and women inevitably preach when they plead with their fellows to be all that they can be. It is a pertinent sermon when the principle of evil is abroad on the earth, and when many of those we love strike awe in us by the majesty with which they surpass themselves in the defense of immortal values.

I prize it as a Book of Remembrance, a study of the art of gratitude. You may find much more in it, but that is enough for me.

JOHN ERSKINE

New York, December 26, 1942

.

INTRODUCTION

I GLADLY accept the translator's invitation to furnish a few words of introduction to Fechner's "Büchlein vom Leben nach dem Tode," the more so as its somewhat oracularly uttered sentences require, for their proper understanding, a certain acquaintance with their relations to his general system.

Fechner's name lives in physics as that of one of the earliest and best determiners of electrical constants, also as that of the best systematic defender of the atomic theory. In psychology it is a commonplace to glorify him as the first user of experimental methods, and the first aimer at exactitude in facts. In cosmology he is known as the author of a system of evolution which, while taking great account of physical details and mechanical conceptions, makes consciousness correlative to and coeval with the whole physical world. In literature he has made his mark by certain half-humoristic, half-philosophic essays published under the name of Dr. Mises—indeed the present booklet originally appeared under that name. In æsthetics he may lay claim to be the earliest systematically empirical student. In metaphysics he is not only the author of an independently reasoned ethical system, but of a theological theory worked out in great detail. His mind, in short, was one of those multitudinously organized cross-roads of truth, which are occupied only at rare intervals by children of men, and from which nothing is either too far or too near to be seen in due perspective. Patient observation and daring imagination dwelt hand in hand in Fechner; and perception, reasoning, and feeling all flourished on the largest scale without interfering either with the other's function.

Fechner was, in fact, a philosopher in the "great" sense of the term, although he cared so much less than most philosophers do for purely logical abstractions. For him the abstract lived in the concrete; and although he worked as definitely and technically as the narrowest specialist works in each of the many lines of scientific inquiry which he successively followed, he followed each and all of them for the sake of his one overmastering general purpose, the purpose namely of elaborating what he called the "day-light-view" of the world into greater and greater system and completeness.

By the daylight-view, as contrasted with the night-view, Fechner meant the anti-materialistic view,—the view that the entire material universe, instead of being dead, is inwardly alive and consciously animated. There is hardly a page of his writing that was not probably connected in his mind with this most general of his interests.

Little by little the materialistic generation that called his speculations fantastic has been replaced by one with greater liberty of imagination. Leaders of thought, a Paulsen, a Wundt, a Preyer, a Lasswitz, treat Fechner's pan-psychism as plausible, and write of its author with veneration. Younger men chime in, and Fechner's philosophy promises to become scientifically fashionable. Imagine a Herbert Spencer who, to the unity of his system and its unceasing touch with facts, should have added a positively religious philosophy instead of Spencer's dry agnosticism; who should have mingled humor and lightness (even though it were germanic lightness) with his heavier ratiocinations; who should have been no less encyclopedic and far more subtle; who should have shown a personal life as simple and as consecrated to the one pursuit of truth,—imagine this, I say, if you can, and you may form some idea of what the name of Fechner is more and more coming to stand for, and of the esteem in which it is more and more held by the studious youth of his native Germany. His belief that the whole material universe is conscious in divers spans and wavelengths, inclusions and envelopments, seems assuredly destined to found a school that will grow more systematic and solidified as time goes on.

The general background of the present dogmatically written little treatise is to be found in the "Tagesansicht," in the "Zend-Avesta," and in various other works of Fechner's. Once grasp the idealistic notion that inner experience is the reality, and that matter is but a form in which inner experiences may appear to one another when they affect each other from the outside; and it is easy to believe that consciousness or inner experience never originated, or developed, out of the unconscious, but that it and the physical universe are co-eternal aspects of one selfsame reality, much as concave and convex are aspects of one curve. "Psychophysical movement," as Fechner

16

calls it, is the most pregnant name for all the reality that is. As "movement" it has a "direction"; as "psychical" the direction can be felt as a "tendency" and as all that lies connected in the way of inner experience with tendencies,—desire, effort, success, for example; while as "physical" the direction can be defined in spatial terms and formulated mathematically or otherwise in the shape of a descriptive "law."

But movements can be superimposed and compounded, the smaller on the greater, as wavelets upon waves. This is as true in the mental as in the physical sphere. Speaking psychologically, we may say that a general wave of consciousness rises out of a subconscious background, and that certain portions of it catch the emphasis, as wavelets catch the light. The whole process is conscious, but the emphatic wave-tips of the consciousness are of such contracted span that they are momentarily insulated from the rest. They realize themselves apart, as a twig might realize itself, and forget the parent tree. Such an insulated bit of experience leaves, however, when it passes away, a memory of itself. The residual and subsequent consciousness becomes different for its having occurred. On the physical side we say that the brain-process that

17

corresponded to it altered permanently the future mode of action of the brain.

Now, according to Fechner, our bodies are just wavelets on the surface of the earth. We grow upon the earth as leaves grow upon a tree, and our consciousness arises out of the whole earth-consciousness, —which it forgets to thank,—just as within our consciousness an emphatic experience arises, and makes us forget the whole background of experience without which it could not have come. But as it sinks again into that background it is not forgotten. On the contrary, it is remembered and, as remembered, leads a freer life, for it now combines, itself a conscious idea, with the innumerable, equally conscious ideas of other remembered things. Even so is it, when we die, with the whole system of our outlived experiences. During the life of our body, although they were always elements in the more general enveloping earth-consciousness, yet they themselves were unmindful of the fact. Now, impressed on the whole earth-mind as memories, they lead the life of ideas there, and realize themselves no longer in isolation, but along with all the similar vestiges left by other human lives, entering with these into new combinations, affected anew by experiences of the living, and affecting the living in their turn, enjoying, in short, that "third stage" of existence with the definition of which the text of the present work begins.

God, for Fechner, is the totalized consciousness of the whole universe, of which the Earth's consciousness forms an element, just as in turn my human consciousness and yours form elements of the whole earth's consciousness. As I apprehend Fechner (though I am not sure), the whole Universe—God therefore also— evolves in time: that is, God has a genuine history. Through us as its human organs of experience the earth enriches its inner life, until it also "geht zu grunde" and becomes immortal in the form of those still wider elements of inner experience which its history is even now weaving into the total cosmic life of God.

The whole scheme, as the reader sees, is got from the fact that the span of our own inner life alternately contracts and expands. You cannot say where the exact outline of any present state of consciousness lies. It shades into a more general background in which even now other states lie ready to be known. This background is the inner aspect of what physically appear, first, as our residual and only partially excited neural elements, and then more remotely as the whole organism which we call our own.

This indetermination of the partition, this fact of a changing threshold, is the analogy which Fechner generalizes, that is all.

There are many difficulties attaching to his theory. The complexity with which he himself realizes them, and the subtlety with which he meets them are admirable. It is interesting to see how closely his speculations, due to such different motives, and supported by such different arguments, agree with those of some of our own philosophers. Royce's Gifford lectures, "The World and the Individual," Bradley's Appearance and Reality, and A. E. Taylor's Elements of "Metaphysics," present themselves immediately to one's mind.

WILLIAM JAMES

Chocorua, N. H., June 21, 1904

LIFE
AFTER
DEATH

CHAPTER ONE

MAN LIVES upon the earth not once, but three times. His first stage of life is a continuous sleep; the second is an alternation between sleeping and waking; the third is an eternal waking.

In the first stage man lives alone in darkness; in the second he lives with companions, near and among others, but detached and in a light which pictures for him the exterior; in the third his life is merged with that of other souls into the higher life of the Supreme Spirit, and he discerns the reality of ultimate things.

In the first stage the body is developed from the germ and evolves its equipment for the second; in the second the spirit unfolds from its seed-bud and realizes its powers for the third; in the third is developed the divine spark which lies in every human soul, and which, already here through perception, faith, feeling, the intuition of Genius, demonstrates the world beyond man—to the soul in the third stage as clear as day, though to us obscure.

The passing from the first to the second stage is called birth; the transition from the second to the third is called death.

The way upon which we pass from the second to the third stage is not darker than that by which we reach the second from the first. The one leads to the outer, the other to the inner aspect of the world.

But as the child in the first stage is still blind and deaf to all the glory and joy of the life of the second, and his birth from the warm body of his mother is hard and painful, with a moment when the dissolution of his earlier existence feels like death, before the awakening to the new environment without has occurred,—so we in our present existence, in which our whole consciousness lies bound in our contracted body, as yet know nothing of the splendor and harmony, the radiance and freedom of the third stage, and easily hold the dark and narrow way which leads us into it as a blind pitfall which has no outlet. But death is only a second birth into a freer existence, in which the spirit breaks through its slender covering and abandons inaction and sloth, as the child does in its first birth.

Then all, which with our present senses only reaches us as exterior and, as it were, from afar, we become penetrated with and possessed of in all its depth of reality. The spirit will no longer wander over mountain and field, or be surrounded by the delights of spring, only to mourn that it all seems exterior to him; but, transcending earthly limitations, he will feel new strength and joy in growing. He will no longer struggle by persuasive words to produce a thought in others, but in the immediate influence of souls upon each other, no longer separated by the body, but united spiritually, he will experience the joy of creative thought; he will not outwardly appear to the loved ones left behind, but will dwell in their inmost souls, and think and act in and through them.

CHAPTER TWO

T HE UNBORN CHILD has merely a corporeal frame, a forming principle. The creation and development of its limbs by which it reaches full growth are its own acts. It has not yet the feeling that these parts are its possession, for it needs them not and cannot use them. A fine eye, a beautiful mouth, are to him only objects to be secured unconsciously, so that they may sometime become serviceable parts of himself. They are made for a subsequent world of which the child as yet knows nothing: it fashions them by virtue of an impulse, blind to him, which is clearly established alone in the organization of the mother.[1]

[1] It may thus be more clearly stated to the physiologist: The creative principle of the child lies, before birth, not in that which after birth will continue to live on with him, which indeed now is only dependence, the product, but in that which at birth will remain behind and be cast off, like the body of man in death (*placenta cum puniculo umbilicali,*

But when the child, ripe for the second stage of life, slips away from the organ representing the provision for his former needs, it leaves it behind, and suddenly sees itself an independent union of all its created parts. This eye, ear, and mouth now belong to him; and even if acquired only through an obscure inborn sense, he is learning to know their precious uses. The world of light, color, tone, perfume, taste, and feeling is only now revealed as the arena in which the functions acquired to that end are to operate for him, if he makes them serviceable and strong.

The relation of the first stage to the second recurs in a higher degree in the relations of the second to the third. Our whole action and will in this world

---

velamentis ovi eorumque liquoribus) : out of its activity emerges, as its continuation, the young human being.

[In the embryonic period it seemed to the child that the placenta was its body, and it was actually its special embryonic body, useless in another stage, and rejected as refuse at the moment of birth. Our body in human life is like a second envelope which is useless to the third life, and for this reason we reject it at the moment of our second birth. Human life as compared with the celestial is truly embryonic.

ELIPHAS LEVI.]

The translator.

is exactly calculated to procure for us an organism, which, in the next world, we shall perceive and use as our Self. All spiritual influences, all results of the manifestations which in the lifetime of a man go forth from him, to be interwoven with humanity and nature, are already united by a secret and invisible bond; they are the spiritual limbs of the man, which he exercises during life while still bound to a spiritual body, to an organism full of unsatisfied, upreaching powers and activities, the consciousness of which still lies outside him, though inseparably interwoven with his present existence, yet, only in abandoning this, can he recognize it as his own.

But in the moment of death, when the man is separated from the organ upon which his acquisitive efforts were bent here, he suddenly receives the consciousness of all, which as a result of his earlier exterior life in the world of ideas, powers, and activities, still survives, prevails, flowing out as from a well-spring, while still bearing also within himself his organic unity.

This, however, now becomes a living, conscious, independent, and, according to his destiny, controls mankind and nature with his own completed individual power.

Whatever any one has contributed during his life, of creation, formation, or preservation, to the sum of human idealism, is his immortal part, which, in the third stage, will continue to operate even if the body, to which, in the second, this working power was bound, were long since destroyed. What millions who have died have acquired, performed, and thought, has not died with them—nor will it be undone by what the next millions shall have acquired, performed, and thought, but continues its power, unfolds itself in them spontaneously, impels them towards a great goal which they do not themselves perceive.

This ideal survival seems indeed to us only an abstraction, and the continued influence of the soul of the dead in the living but an empty fancy.

But it only appears so to us because we have no power to perceive in them spirits in the third stage, to comprehend a predestined and permanent existence; we can only recognize the connecting link of their existence with ours, the portion of increase within us, appearing under the form of those ideas which have been transmitted from them to us. Although the undulating circle which a sinking stone leaves behind it in the water creates, by its contact, a new circle around every rock which still projects above the surface, it still retains in itself a connected circumference which stirs and carries all within its reach; but the rocks are only aware of the breaking of the perfect line. We are just such ignorant objects, only that we, unlike fixed rocks, while even still in life, shed about us a continuous flow of influence which extends itself not only around others but within them.

Already, in fact, during his lifetime, every man with his influence grows into others through word, example, writing, and deed. While Goethe lived, contemporary millions bore within them sparks from his soul, and were thereby newly kindled. In Napoleon's life nearly the whole period was penetrated by the force of his spirit. With their death these tributary sources of life did not also die; only the motive power of a new earth-born channel expired, and the growth and manifestation of this, emanating from an individual, and in their totality again forming an individual, production now takes place with a similar indwelling consciousness, incomprehensible indeed to us, as was its first inception. A Goethe, a Schiller, a Napoleon, a Luther, still live among us, thinking and acting in us, as awakened creative individuals, more highly developed than at their death—each no longer restrained by the limitations of the body, but poured forth upon the world which in their lifetime they moulded, gladdened, swayed, and in their personality far surpassing the influences which we still discern as coming from them.

The greatest example of a mighty soul which still lives on actively in after-ages is Christ. It is not an empty saying that Christ lives on in his followers; every true Christian holds him not only relatively but absolutely within his heart. Every one is a partaker in him who acts and thinks in obedience to his law, for it is the Christ that prompts this thinking and acting in each. He has extended his influence through all the members of his Church and all cling together through his Spirit, like the apple to its stem, the branches to the vine. "For as the body is one, and hath many members, and all the members of that one body, being many, are one body: so also is Christ." (1 Cor. xii.

12.[1]) Yet not only the greatest souls, but every strong man awakes in the next world in conscious though incomplete possession of an organism which is a union of eternal spiritual acquirements and influences, with a greater or smaller extent of realization, and more or less power to unfold further, according as the soul of the man himself in his lifetime has advanced and gained ground. But he who has clung to the earth, and has only used his powers in pursuit of the material life, the pleasures and needs of the body, will find but an insignificant remnant of life surviving. And so the richest will become the poorest if he has only his gold to lean upon, and the poorest the richest if he uses his strength to win his life honestly. For what each does here he will have there, and money there will only count for what it brought the consumer here.

The problems of our present spiritual life, the thirst for the discovery of truth, which here seems to profit us but little, the striving of every genuine soul to accomplish things which are merely for the good of posterity, conscience, and the repentance that arouses

[1] Many biblical parallels similar to this are placed together in Zend-Avesta III. p. 363, and "Drei Motive und Gründe des Glaubens," p. 178.

in us an unfathomable distress for bad actions, even though they bring us no disadvantage here, rise from haunting presentiments of what all this will bring to us in that world in which the fruit of our slightest and most hidden activity becomes a part of our true self.

This is the great justice of creation, that every one makes for himself the conditions of his future life. Deeds will not be requited to the man through exterior rewards or punishments; there is no heaven and no hell in the usual sense of the Christian, the Jew, the heathen, into which the soul may enter after death. It makes neither a spring upward nor a fall downward, nor comes to a standstill; it does not break asunder, nor dissolve into the universal; but, after it has passed through the great transition, death, it unfolds itself according to the unalterable law of nature upon earth; steadily advancing step by step, and quietly approaching and entering into a higher existence. And, according as the man has been good or bad, has behaved nobly or basely, was industrious or idle, will he find himself possessed of an organism, healthy or sick, beautiful or hateful, strong or weak, in the world to come, and his free activity in this world will determine his relation to other souls, his destiny, his capacity and talents for further progress in that world.

Therefore be active and brave. For the idler here will halt there, the earthbound will be of a dull and weak countenance, and the false and wicked will feel the discord which his presence makes in the company of true and pure spirits as a pain, which, even in that world, will still impel him to amend and cure the evil which he has committed in this, and will allow him no peace nor rest until he has wiped out and atoned for his smallest and latest evil deed.

And if his companion spirits have for long rested in God, or rather lived as partakers in His thoughts, he will still be pursued by the tribulation and restlessness of the earthly life, and his spiritual disorder will torment men with ideas of error and superstition, lead them into vice and folly, and while he himself is retarded on his way to achievement in the third stage, he also will hold back those in whom he survives, upon their path from the second to the third.

But however long the false, the evil, and the base may still prevail and struggle for its life with the true, the beautiful, and the good,—yet through the ever-increasing power of truth, and the growing force of evil's own self-destructive results, it will at last be conquered and abolished; and so of all falsehood, all evil, all impurity in the soul of man, there will at last be nothing left. That alone is the eternal, imperishable part of a man that is to him true, beautiful, and good. And if only a grain of mustard-seed of it is in him—there could be no one without it—so, purged of chaff and dross through the purgatory of life, afflicting only the imperfect, it will survive in the third stage, and, even if late, be able to grow into a noble tree.

Rejoice then, even you whose soul is here tried by tribulation and sorrow; the discipline will avail much, which in the brave struggle with obstacles in the path of progress you have experienced in this life, and, born into the new life with more strength, you will more quickly and joyfully recover what fate has denied you here.

CHAPTER THREE

MAN USES many means to one end; God one means to many ends.

The plant thinks it is in its place for its own purpose, to grow, to toss in the wind, to drink in light and air, to prepare fragrance and color for its own adornment, to play with beetles and bees. It is indeed there for itself, but at the same time it is only one pore of the earth, in which light, air, and water meet and mingle in processes important to the whole earthly life; it is there in order that the earth may exhale, breathe, weave for itself a green garment and provide nourishment, raiment and warmth for men and animals. Man thinks that he is in his place for himself alone, for amusement, for work, and getting his bodily and mental growth; he, too, is indeed there for himself; but his body and mind are also but a dwelling place into which new and higher impulses enter, mingle, and develop, and engage in all sorts of processes together, which both constitute the feeling and thinking of the man, and have their higher meaning for the third stage of life.

The mind of man is alike indistinguishably his own possession and that of the higher intelligences, and what proceeds from it belongs equally to both always, but in different ways. Just as in this figure, which is

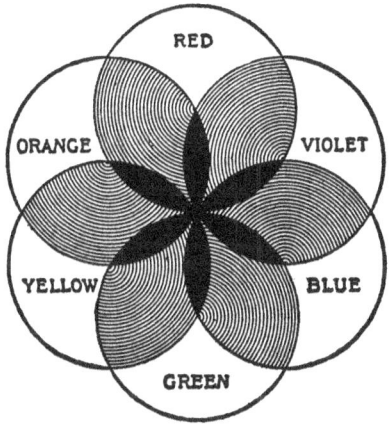

intended not for a representation but only a symbol, the central, colored, six-rayed star (looking black here) can be considered as independent and having unity in itself; its rays proceeding from the middle point are all thereby dependently and harmoniously bound together; on the other hand, it appears again mingled together from the concatenation of the six single colored circles, each one of which has its own individuality. And as each of its rays belongs as well to it as to the circles, through the overlapping of which it is formed, so is it with the human soul.

Man does not often know from whence his thoughts come to him: he is seized with a longing, a foreboding, or a joy, which he is quite unable to account for; he is urged to a force of activity, or a voice warns him away from it, without his being conscious of any special cause. These are the visitations of spirits, which think and act in him from another centre than his own. Their influence is even more manifest in us, when, in abnormal conditions (clairvoyance or mental disorder) the really mutual relation of dependence between them and us is determined in their favor, so that we only passively receive what flows into us from them, without return on our part.

But so long as the human soul is awake and healthy, it is not the weak plaything or product of the spirits which grow into it or of which it appears to be made up, but precisely that which unites these spirits, the invisible centre, possessing primitive living energy, full of spiritual power of attraction, in which all unite, intersect, and through mutual communication engender thoughts in each other, this is not brought into being by the mingling of the spirits, but is inborn in man at his birth; and free will, self-determination, consciousness, reason, and the foundation of all spiritual power are contained herein. But at birth all this lies still latent within, like an unopened seed, awaiting development into an organism full of vital individual activity.

So when man has entered into life other spirits perceive it and press forward from all sides and seek to add his strength to theirs in order to reinforce their own power, but while this is successful, their power becomes at the same time the possession of the human soul itself, is incorporated with it and assists its development.

The outside spirits established within a man are quite as much subjected to the influence of the human will, though in a different way, as man is dependent upon them; he can, from the centre of his spiritual being, equally well produce new growth in the spirits united to him within, as these can definitely influence his deepest life; but in harmoniously developed spiritual life no one will has the mastery over another. As every outside spirit has only a part of itself in common with a single human being, so can the will of the single man have a suggestive influence alone upon a spirit which with its whole remaining part lies outside the man; and since every human mind contains within itself something in common with widely differing outside spirits, so too can the will of a single one among them have only a quickening influence upon the whole man, and only when he, with free choice, wholly denies himself to single spirits is he deprived of the capacity to master them.

All spirits cannot be united indiscriminately in the same soul; therefore the good and bad, the true and false spirits contend together for possession of it, and the one who conquers in the struggle holds the ground.

The interior discord which so often finds place in men is nothing but this conflict of outside spirits who wish to get possession of his will, his reason, in short, his whole innermost being. As the man feels the agreement of spirits within him as rest, clearness, harmony, and safety, he is also conscious of their discord as unrest, doubt, vacillation, confusion, enmity, in his heart. But not as a prize won without effort, or as a willing victim, does he fall to the stronger spirits in this contest, but, with a source of self-active strength in the centre of his being, he stands between the contending forces within which wish to draw him to themselves, and fights on whichever side he chooses; and so he can carry the day even for the weaker impulses, when he joins his strength to theirs against the stronger. The Self of the man remains unendangered so long as he preserves the inborn freedom of his power and does not become tired of using it. As often, however, as he becomes subject to evil spirits, is it because the development of his interior strength is hindered by discouragement, and so, to become bad, it is often only necessary to be careless and lazy.

The better the man already is, the easier it is for him to become still better; and the worse he is, so much the more easily is he quite ruined. For the good man has already harbored many good spirits, which are now associated with him against the evil ones remaining and those freshly pressing for entrance, and are saving for him his interior strength. The good man does good without weariness, his spirits do it for him; but the bad man must first overcome and subdue by his own will all the evil spirits which have striven against him. Moreover, kin seeks and unites itself to kin, and flees from its opposite when not forced. Good spirits in us attract good spirits outside us, and the evil spirits in us the evil outside. Pure spirits turn gladly to enter a pure soul, and evil without fastens upon the evil within. If only the good spirits in our souls have gained the upper hand, so of itself the last devil still remaining behind in us flees away, he is not secure in good society; and so the soul of a good man becomes a pure and heavenly abiding place for happy indwelling spirits. But even good spirits, if they despair of winning a soul from the final mastery of evil, desert it, and so it becomes at last a hell, a place fit only for the torments of the damned. For the agony of conscience and the inner desolation and unrest in the soul of the wicked are sorrows which, not they alone, but the condemned spirits within them also, feel in still deeper woe.

CHAPTER FOUR

W HILE THE higher spirits not only dwell in individual men, but each extends itself into many, it is they who unite these men spiritually, whether of one form of faith or truth, of one moral or political leaning. All men who have any spiritual fellowship with each other belong to the body of one and the same spirit together, and follow the ideal which has thereby been born within them, as members one of another. Often an idea lives at one time in a whole nation, often is a mass of men moved to one and the same action; that is a mighty spirit which seizes them all in one contagious influence. Not alone, indeed, through the spirits of the dead do these alliances occur, but countless new-born ideas flow from the living to the living; all these ideas, however, which go forth from the living into the world are already parts of its future spiritual organism.

Now when two kindred spirits meet in human life

and are merged together through their common sentiments, while simultaneously, through their differing traits, they mutually influence and enrich each other, at the same time the associations, races, nations, to which each first belonged, enter into spiritual association and enrich each other through their spiritual possessions. So the development of the third stage of life in mankind goes on hand in hand inseparably with that of the progress of humanity. The gradual formation of the state, of sciences, of the arts, of human intercourse, the growth of this sphere of life to an ever-increasing harmoniously constructed whole, is the result of this union of innumerable spiritual individualities which live in humanity and fashion it into great spiritual organisms.

How otherwise could these glorious realms, based upon such unalterable principles, be formed out of the tangled egotism of individuals, who, with their short-sighted eyes, from the centre could see no circumference, and at the circumference could discern no centre, if the higher spirits, seeing clearly through the whole, did not control the machinery, and, while they all press around the common divine centre, and so in

44

their godlike part meet together, also lead the men whom they influenced, united on to higher goals.

But beside the harmony of spirits which meet and fraternize amicably, there is also a conflict of those whose existence is in disagreement, a struggle which will at last wear itself out, so that the eternal in its purity shall alone survive. Traces of this warring of forces are manifested by mankind in the rivalry of systems, in sectarian hatred, in wars and revolutions between princes and people, and the nations among each other.

The mass of men enter into all these great spiritual movements with blind faith, blind obedience, blind hatred and rage; they hear and see nothing with their own spiritual ears and eyes; they are driven by alien spirits toward objects and goals of which they themselves know nothing; they allow themselves to be led through slavery, death, and terrible affliction, like a flock following the call of the higher leadership.

There are, indeed, men who engage in this great agitation, acting and leading with clear consciousness and deep purpose. But they are only voluntary means to great predestined ends; being able, indeed, through their free action to determine the quality and rapidity,

45

but not the goal of progress. Those only have had great influence in the world who have recognized the spiritual tendency of the time in which they lived and have directed their free action and thought into that tendency: equally strong men who have resisted it have been overthrown. Every one who has set before him higher aims, and knows better ways thither, has chosen a new central point for his motive power; not as a blind tool, but as one who from his own impulse and understanding serves righteousness and wisdom. The brow-beaten slave does not render the best service. But in whatever way men begin to serve God here they will carry further there, as partakers of His divine glory.

46

CHAPTER FIVE

I T IS, INDEED, possible for the spirits of the living and the dead to meet unconsciously in many ways, and also consciously only on one side. Who can pursue and trace out this whole line of communication? Let us say briefly: they meet together when in mutual consciousness, and the dead are present whereever they are so consciously.

One means there is of attaining the highest conscious meeting between the living and the dead; it is the memory of the living for the dead. To direct our attention to the dead is to awaken theirs to us, just as a charm which is found in a living person encourages a corresponding attraction toward the one perceiving it.

Although our memory of the dead is but a new consciousness, in retrospect, of the results of their known life here, yet the life on the other side will be led conformably to that in this world.

Even when one living person thinks of another, a conscious mutual impulse may be aroused: but it is inoperative because of the still present confines of the body. Once released, however, by death, that consciousness seeks its own realm and is then borne upon a current the more swift and strong, as it has previously been exerted and manifested with frequency and power.

Now just as one and the same physical blow is felt at the same time by the giver and the receiver, so is it but a single shock of consciousness that is experienced on both sides when one recalls the dead to memory. Realizing alone this earthly side of consciousness, we err because we fail to discern the other: and this failure brings results of error and loss.

One beloved person is parted from another, a wife from a husband, a mother from a child. In vain do they search in a distant heaven the part of their lives that has been torn from them; in vain they reach out into the void with eye and hand after that which in reality has never been taken away from them; because out of the exterior relations of mutual adjustment and understanding, the threads of which are now broken, has sprung out of the depths of interior consciousness

48

a deep and unobstructed union, as yet unfamiliar and unrecognized.

I saw once a mother anxiously seeking through garden and house for her living child which she was carrying in her arms. Still more mistaken is he who seeks for his dead in a remote and deserted place, when he had but to look within to find him still present. And if she does not find him wholly there, did the mother then completely possess her child even while she was carrying him in her arms? The satisfactions of the outward relations, the spoken word, the glance of the eye, the personal care, she can no more have or give; now for the first time she has those of the inner life; she must simply recognize that there is such an interior relation with its advantages. No word is spoken, no hand extended to the one who we think is not present. But if we knew all, a new life is to begin for the living and the dead, and the dead gain thereby as well as the living.

If we think of the dead rightly, not merely holding him in mind, he is at that moment present. If you can deeply summon him, he must come, if you hold him fast, he must remain, if sense and thought are strong enough to bind and retain him. And he will perceive

49

whether we think of him with love or with hatred; and the stronger the love or the stronger the hatred, the more clearly he will discern it. Once, indeed, you had a remembrance of the dead—now you are able to use that remembrance; you can still knowingly bless or torment the dead with your memories, be reconciled to them or remain in a state of conflict—not alone consciously to you but also to them. Have the best constantly in mind, and be careful only that the memory that you yourself are to leave behind shall be a blessing to you in the future. Well for him who leaves behind him a treasure of love, esteem, honor, and admiration in the memory of men. Such enrichment is his gain in death, since he acquires the condensed consciousness of the whole earthly estimate concerning him; he grasps in full measure the bushel, of which in life he could count but a few kernels. This belongs to the treasure which we are to lay up in heaven.

Woe to him who is followed by execration, cursing, and a memory full of dread. Those whom he influenced in this life will not release him in death; this belongs to the hell which is awaiting him. Every reproach that pursues him is like an arrow which, with sure aim, enters into his inmost soul.

But only in the totality of results which evolves itself from good and evil alike is justice fulfilled. The righteous who were here misunderstood must inevitably suffer from it there as from a misfortune; and to the unrighteous an unjust reputation will serve as an outward advantage; therefore, keep your good name as pure as possible here below and "hide not thy light under a bushel." But among the spirits in that other sphere even misunderstanding shall cease; what was here held as false shall there be found true and by increase be given additional weight. Divine justice overcomes at last all human injustice.

Whatever awakens the memory of the dead is a means of calling them to us.

At every festival which we devote to them they rise up; they float about every monument which we raise to them; they listen to every song with which we praise their deeds. A life germ for a new art! How antiquated had these old dramas become, produced over and over again to the weary spectators. Now all at once, above the ground floor with its expanse of old onlookers, there is revealed, as it were, an encircling realm from which a higher company is seen to be looking down, and straightway it becomes the highest aim of men to grow into the likeness of those above rather than those below, to realize, not the desires of those below, but of those above.

The scoffers scoff and the churches contend. It is a question of a secret, irrational to some, rational to others, both because to one and the other a greater mystery remains unrevealed, from the disclosure of which comes quite clearly and obviously the rock upon which the mind of the scoffer and the unity of the church have been wrecked. For it is only a supreme example of a universal law in which they discern an exception to and above all laws.

Not alone through the consecrated bread and wine does Christ reach His followers at the Holy Supper; partake of it in pure remembrance of Him, and He, with His thought, will be not only with you, but in you; the more deeply, as you hold Him more closely in your heart; the more vitally, with so much the more strength will He fortify you; yet, without communion with Him, the sacrament remains but meal and water and common wine.

CHAPTER SIX

THE LONGING in every man to meet again after death those who were most dear to him here, to have communication with them, renewing the old relations, will be satisfied in a more perfect degree than was ever anticipated or hoped for.

For in that life those who were united here by a common spiritual bond will not only meet but will have become one through this bond; there will be for them a unified soul belonging with a common consciousness to both. For already, indeed, are the dead with the living, as are the living themselves bound together by countless such common ties; but only when death loosens the knot and removes the body which envelops every living soul, will there be added to the union of consciousness the consciousness of union.

Every one in the moment of death will perceive that he still has a place and belongs in the company with those gone before, from whom through common interests he has received help, and so will not enter into the third world as a strange guest, but like one long expected, to whom all with whom he was here united through a common faith, knowledge, and love, will stretch out their hands to draw him to themselves as a partaker of their existence.

Into similar deep fellowship shall we also enter with those great dead who long before our time wandered through the second stage of life, and upon whose example and teaching our own spirit was moulded. So, whoever here lived wholly in Christ will there be also wholly in Him. Yet his individuality will not be extinguished in the higher one, but only gain in power from it, and at the same time reinforce the strength of the higher. For those souls which have grown together as one through their moments of sympathy, gain force each from the other for itself, and at the same time confirmation as individuals through the union of their diversities.

So, many souls will mutually strengthen each other in the greater part of their nature; others are connected only by a few corresponding qualities.

Not all these ties based upon certain spiritual experiences in common will be permanent, but they will be so when they are within the realm of truth, beauty, and virtue.

All that does not bear within itself eternal harmony, even if it survives this life, will yet at last come to naught and will cause a separation of those souls which for a time had been united in an unworthy alliance.

Most spiritual perceptions which are developed in the present life, and which we take over into the next, bear, it is true, a germ of truth, goodness, and virtue within themselves, but enveloped in a large addition of unessential falseness, error, and corruption. Those spirits which remain united through such impulses may so continue or they may separate, according as they both agree to hold fast to the good and the best, and to abandon the evil by their separation from evil spirits, or according as one seizes on the good and the other on the evil.

Those souls, however, which have seized together upon a form or an idea of truth, beauty, or goodness in their eternal purity, remain thereby united to all eternity and in like manner possess these ideals as a part of themselves in everlasting unity.

The comprehension of the higher thought by advanced souls means therefore their growth through this thought into greater spiritual organisms, and as all individual ideas have their root in the universal, so at last will all souls, in fellowship with the highest, be absorbed into the divine.

The spiritual world in its consummation will therefore be, not an assembly, but a tree of souls, the root of which is planted on earth and whose summit reaches to the heavens.

Only the highest and noblest spirits, Christ, the geniuses, the saints, are able to reach, out of their full knowledge, the centre of divinity face to face; the smaller and lesser ones have their roots in these, as boughs in branches and twigs in boughs, and are thus connected midway indirectly through them with the highest of the high.

And so dead geniuses and saints are the true mediators between God and man; partaking of the thought of God they are able to convey it to man, and at the same time feeling and understanding human sorrows, joys, and desires, they are able to lead him to God.

Yet the worship of the dead stands in relation to the deified worship of nature, at the very beginning of religion, half related and half separated; the most savage nations have retained it in its cruder, the most civilized in its higher form. And where to-day is there one which does not preserve a large fragment of it as its corner-stone?

And so there should be in every town a shrine for its greatest dead, built near or in the temple of God, and let Christ as heretofore dwell in the same temple as God himself.

CHAPTER SEVEN

For NOW we see through a glass, darkly; but then face to face: now I know in part; but then shall I know even as also I am known."—1 Cor. xiii. 12.

Man lives here at once an outer and an inner life, the first all visible and audible in look, word, writing, in outward affairs and works, the last perceptible to himself only through interior thoughts and feelings. The continuation of the visible into the exterior is easily followed; the development of the unseen remains itself invisible, but yet goes on. Rather the inner life of man progresses, with his outer life, as its nucleus, to form the nucleus of the future life.

In fact, that which goes out visibly and perceptibly from man during his lifetime is not the only thing that emanates from him. However small and fine the vibration or impulse may be by which a conscious emotion is carried to our minds, yet the whole play of conscious emotions is borne by an inward mental ac-

58

tion, it cannot die out without producing effects of its kind in us and at last beyond us; only we cannot follow them into life outside. As little as can the lute keep its playing to itself, it is borne out beyond it, so little can our minds; to the lute or the mind belongs only that which is closest to it. What an infinitely complex play of subtle waves having their origin in our minds may spread itself over the gross lower realm of action, perceptible to the outward eye and ear, like the fine ripples on the large waves of a pond, or the flat designs on the surface of a closely woven carpet, which takes from them its whole beauty and higher meaning. The physicist, however, recognizes and follows only the action of the lower exterior order, and does not concern himself with the finer, which he does not perceive. But even if he does not perceive it, yet knowing the principle, does he dare deny the result?[1]

[1] Whether one attributes nervous energy to a chemical or an electrical process, one must still regard it, if not simply as the play of the vibration of minutest atoms, yet as in the main excited or accompanied by this, whereby the imponderable has a larger part than the ponderable. Vibrations, however, can only apparently expire by extending themselves into their environment, or if indeed they disappear for a time through translation of their living strength into so-called elasticity,

59

Therefore, what we have absorbed from souls through the influences of their outward perceptible life in this world does not yet comprise their whole being; but, in a way incomprehensible to us, there still remains in their nature, besides that outward part, a deeper, indeed the chief part of their existence. And if a man had spent and ended his life on a desert island without ever having come in contact with another human life, he would have firmly retained his inner existence, awaiting a future development, which in this world he could not find through intercourse with others. If on the other hand a child had lived but a moment, it could not die again in eternity. The least impulse of conscious life surrounds itself with a circle of influences, just as the briefest tone, which in a moment seems to die, throws out vibrations which reach out into infinity, beyond those standing near by and listening; for no influence expires in itself, and each produces others of its kind into eternity. And so will the soul of the child go on developing from this conscious beginning like that of the man left in isolation,

---

yet, according to the law of the conservation of energy, they await a revival in some other form.

only otherwise than as if beginning from an already advanced development.

Now, just as man in death first receives the full consciousness of what he has produced spiritually in others, so also in death will he acquire for the first time complete knowledge and use of what he has cultivated in himself. Whatever he has gathered during life of spiritual treasure, what fills his memory or penetrates his feeling, what his intelligence and imagination have created, remain forever his! Yet its whole connection remains dark in this life; thought merely passes through with a light-giving ray and illuminates what lies on the narrow line of his life, the rest remaining in obscurity. The soul here below never realizes all at once the entire depth of its fulness; only when one of its impulses draws another into union with itself does it emerge for an instant from the darkness, only to sink back again in the next. So man is a stranger to his own soul and wanders about within it as he may, or wearily seeking the way to his life's end, and often forgets his best treasures, which, aside from the glowing path of thought, lie sunken in the darkness which covers the wide region of his soul. But in the moment of death, in which an eternal night darkens the eye of his body, light will begin to dawn in his soul. Then will the centre of the inner man kindle into a sun which illuminates his whole spiritual nature, and at the same time penetrates it as with an inner eye, with divine clearness. All which was here forgotten will he recover there, indeed he only forgot it here because it went before him into the other world; now he finds it again collected. In that new universal luminousness he will no longer be obliged to seek out wearily what he would fain appropriate, separating his own from what he must reject, but at a glance he is able to understand himself wholly, and at the same time to perceive the true relations between unity and diversity, connection and separation, harmony and discord, not only according to one line of thought but equally according to all.[1] As far as are the flight and vision of the bird above the slow crawling of the blind worm which perceives nothing beyond what its slug-

[1] Even in this world, at the approach of death (by narcotics, in imminent drowning, or in exaltation) there occur flashes of recognition of the spiritual meaning of things, examples of which are recorded in Zend-Avesta III. p. 27, and (cases of threatened drowning) in Fechner's Centralblatt für Naturwiss. und Anthropologie, 1853, p. 43 and 623.

gish body touches, so greatly will the higher knowledge transcend that of the present. And so in death, with the body of man will also pass away his mind, his understanding, indeed the whole finite dwelling-place of his soul, as forms become too narrow for its existence, as parts which are of no further use in an order of things in which all knowledge which they had to seek and discover gradually, laboriously, and imperfectly, he now has openly revealed, possessed, and enjoyed. The self of man, however, will subsist unimpaired in its full extent and development through the destruction of its transitory forms, and, in the place of that extinct lower sphere of activity, will enter into a higher life. Stilled is all restlessness of thought, which no longer needs to seek in order to find itself, or to approach another to come into conscious mutual relations. Rather begins now a higher interchange of spiritual life; as in our own minds thoughts interchange together, so between advanced souls there is a fellowship, the all-embracing centre of which we call God, and the play of our thoughts is but tributary to this high communion. Speech will no longer be needed there for mutual understanding, and no eye for recognition of others, but as thought in us comprehends and relates itself to thought, without the medium of ear, mouth, or hand, unites or separates without exterior restraint or prohibition, so comforting, intimate, and untrammelled will mutual spiritual communication be, and nothing will remain hidden in one from the other. All sinful thoughts which here slink away into the dark places of the mind, and all which man would be glad to cover up from his kind with a thousand hands, become known to all. And only the soul which has been quite pure and true here can without shame come into the presence of others in that world; and he who has been misunderstood here on earth will there find recognition.

And even in its individual life will the soul through self-inspection become aware of every deficiency and every remnant, left behind from this life, of imperfection, disturbance, and discord, and not only will it recognize these defects, but feel them, all in common, with the same force as we our bodily infirmities. But as thoughts can be cleansed from all that is unworthy, and in moments of insight be united to still higher thoughts, each becoming thereby perfected in that which was lacking, even so will souls in their mutual intercourse find the path of progress towards perfection.

64

CHAPTER EIGHT

URING HIS lifetime man has not only spiritual but also material relations with nature.

Heat, air, water, and earth press upon him from all sides, and go out from him back again, creating and transforming his body; but as these elements, which outside of man only operate side by side, meet and mingle in him, they form a combination, that of man's bodily sensation, and at once this bodily sensation cuts off man's inner being from the sensations of the outer world. Only through the windows of the senses is man able to look out from his bodily frame and realize the outer world and, as it were, in small handfuls to draw something from it.

But when man dies, with the destruction of his body that combination is loosened, and, released from its bondage to it, the soul will now return to nature with full freedom. He will no longer be conscious of the waves of light and sound only as they strike eye and ear, but, as the waves roll forth into the sea of ether and the sea of air, he will not merely feel the blowing of the wind and the wash of the waves against his body, but will himself murmur in the air and sea; no more wander outwardly through verdant woods and meadows, but himself consciously pervade both wood and meadow and those wandering there.

Therefore nothing is lost to him in the transition to the higher stage, except implements, the limited use of which he can dispense with in an existence in which he will carry and perceive within himself fully and directly all which in the lower stage came to him only fitfully and superficially through their dull mediation. Why should we take over into the life to come eye or ear to obtain light and sound from the spring of living nature, when the current of our future life will merge as one with the waves of light and sound? Even more!

The human eye is only a little radiant spot upon the earth, and only gets the impression in the firmament of points of light. Man's longing to know more of the universe is not here gratified.

He discovers the telescope and magnifies with it the

surface, and so the capacity of his eye; in vain, the stars still remain little points.

Now he believes that he will attain in the next world what this life cannot grant, the final satisfaction of his curiosity; that once in heaven he will immediately perceive all that has been hidden from his earthly eyes.

He is right; but he does not reach a heaven because he receives wings to fly from one planet to another or even into an unseen heaven over the visible one; where in the nature of things could wings exist to that end? He does not learn to know the whole universe, by being slowly borne from one planet to another in ever-repeated birth; no stork is there to carry children from one star to another;—his eye does not gain the capacity for the infinite ethereal depths by being made into a great telescope; the principle of earthly sight will no longer suffice;—yet he will attain to all, in that, as a conscious part of the other life in the great heavenly existence that holds him, he wins a place in its high fellowship with other divinely illuminated beings. A new vision! Not for us here below, because no one of us has reached that plane. In the firmament the earth itself swims like a great eye wholly immersed in the vast star spaces, and swinging around therein, to receive from all sides the impact of waves which cross each other millions and millions of times and yet cause no disturbance. With this eye will man some time learn to discern the heavens, while the forward surging of his future life, with which he pierces it, meets and presses against the wave of the surrounding ether, and with finest pulsations penetrates the universe. Learn to see! And how much will man have to learn after death! For he must not think that, at the first entrance, he will possess the whole divine perception for which the future life will offer him the means. Even here the child first learns to see and hear; for what he sees and hears in the beginning is uncomprehended appearance, is mere sound without meaning—at first indeed only bewilderment, astonishment, and confusion; and nothing different does the new life offer to the new child at first. Only what man brings with him from this life, the composite echo of memories of all he has done and thought and been here, does he see, in the transition, all at once clearly lighted up within itself, yet still he remains primarily only what he was. Neither does any one think that the glory of the other world shall result otherwise to the

68

foolish, the idle, and the bad, than to make them feel the discord of their lives, and to emphasize the necessity for reform. Already in the present life man brings with him an eye to behold the whole glory of heaven and earth, an ear to hear music and the speech of man, an understanding to grasp the meaning of all this; what does it avail to the foolish, the indolent, and the bad?

As the best and the highest in this life so is also the best and the highest in the other only there for the best and the highest, because alone by such understood, wished for, and acquired. Therefore, the higher man of the next world alone can gain a comprehension of the conscious intercourse in the existence into which he has passed with other divine beings, entering with them himself into this fellowship.

Who knows whether the whole earth, revolving in an ever slowly narrowing orbit, will not return to the heart of the sun from which it came, after eons of years, and then a sun life of all earthly creatures will begin; and where is the need of our knowing this now?

CHAPTER NINE

SPIRITS OF the third stage will dwell, as in a common body, in the earthly nature, of which mankind itself is a part, and all natural processes will be the same to them as they are to us in our bodies. Their substance will encompass the forms of the second stage as a common mother, just as those of the second stage surrounded those of the first.

Every soul of the third stage appropriates as its own share of the universal body only what it in the earthly realm has developed and accomplished. What a man has changed in this world by his life in it, that constitutes his further life in the universal existence.

This consists partly of definite accomplishments and deeds, partly of actions continuously recurring, just as the earthly body is made up of fixed parts and of parts which are movable and supported by the fixed ones.

All life circles of the higher spirits intersect each

other, and you ask how it is possible that such num-
berless circles can intersect without disturbance, error,
or confusion.

Ask rather first, how it is possible that innumerable
undulations in the same pond, waves of sound in the
same air, waves of light in the same ether, pulses of
memory in the same mind intersect, that, finally, the
countless life circles of man, bearing their great
future, already in this life intersect without disturbance, error, or confusion. Rather a far higher plane
of life and growth is achieved through these vibrations and memories reaching from this present life to
the one beyond.

But what separates the circles of consciousness
which cross each other?

Nothing separates them in any of those details in
which they cross each other; they have all characteris-
tics in common; only each stands in different relations
from the other; that separates them in general and
distinguishes them in their higher individuality. Ask
again what distinguishes or separates circles which intersect; nothing separately; yet you easily observe an
outward difference yourself in general; still more

easily will centres which are themselves self-conscious also distinguish an inner difference.

Perhaps you have sometimes received from a distant place a letter written across both ways. How do you decipher both writings? Only by the coherence which each has in itself. In like manner is crossed the spiritual handwriting with which the page of the world is filled; and each is read by itself, as if it occupied the whole space, and the others, too, which overlie it. Not merely two, but innumerable letterings make a network of record on the earth; the letter, however, is but an inadequate symbol of the world.

Still, how can consciousness continue to preserve its unity in so large an extension of its ground, how withstand the law of the threshold of consciousness? [1]

[1] This empirical law of the relation between body and soul consists in the fact that consciousness everywhere ceases, if the bodily activity upon which it depends sinks below a certain degree of strength, which is called the threshold. Now in proportion as it extends itself more widely, can it the more easily, on account of the accompanying weakness, fall below this level. As the total consciousness has its threshold, which makes the dividing line between sleeping and waking in the whole man, so, too, is it with the details of consciousness, whence it comes that during waking now this, now that idea

Ask first, how it can preserve its unity in the smaller expanse of the body, of which the larger one is only the continuation. Is, then, your body, is your brain a point? Or is there a central spot within as seat of the soul? No.[1] As it is now the nature of the soul to maintain the limited composite of your body, so in the future will it be to unite the greater composite of the greater body. The divine spirit knits together, indeed, the whole fabric of the world;—or would you seek even for God in one point? In that other world you will only acquire a larger part of His omnipresence.

If you fear that the wave of your future life will not in its extension reach the threshold which here it surmounts, remember that it does not spread itself into an empty world,—then, indeed, would it sink helplessly into an abyss,—but into a realm, which, as the eternal foundation of God, at the same time be-

presents itself or sinks out of sight, according as the particular activity upon which it depends rises above or sinks below the special threshold. (Compare "Elemente der Psychophysik," Kap. 10, 38, 39, and 42.)

[1] Concerning this, compare "Elemente der Psychophysik," Kap. 37, and "Atomenlehre," Kap. 26.

comes the foundation of your life, for only in virtue of the divine life is the creature able to live at all.[1]

So a wren upon the back of an eagle can easily soar above a mountain-top, for which task he himself would be too weak, and at last, from the back of the eagle, fly still a bit higher than the eagle has flown with him. But God is the great eagle as He is the little bird.

[1] In order not to permit an apparent contradiction of the above-mentioned speculation to the psychophysical doctrine of the combined-threshold (upon which the most enlightening word is in Wundt's philos. Stud., IV, p. 204 and 211), note the following: If the psychophysical life-wave (to continue the use of this concise expression) of man, made up of components of the most manifold sort, should spread out into a world which contained only different components, then, indeed, must it be assumed that it, in its extension, would fall below the combined-threshold here under consideration. Since, however, the psychophysical undulatory sea of the universe, among its other components, comprehends also such as are like to those of the human life-wave, and indeed of the most varying height or intensity, therefore such as already rise above or come near the level of the combined-threshold and are only raised still higher by the similar ones which join them, so is the result of the above speculation placed on a somewhat more solid basis. (Note to the third edition.)

How can man after the death of the body do without his brain, so marvellously constructed, that contained every impulse of his mind, that carried the further evolution of those impulses into still greater strength and fulness? Was it formed in vain?

Ask the plant how it can do without the seed, when it bursts from it to grow into the light, that wonderful creation which, through the impulsion of its inner germ, builds itself still further from within. Was it created for nothing?

Where, indeed, can be found a structure so wonderful as your brain, to replace it in the other world, and where, indeed, is there one that surpasses it; yet the future brain will surely transcend this present one.

But is not your whole body a finer and more highly organized creation than eye, ear, brain?—not beyond each part? So, and unspeakably more, the world, of which mankind with its state, its knowledge, art, and traffic is but a part, exceeds your little brain, the part of this part. If you would rise to a higher point of view, only see in the earth, not merely a ball of dry earth, air, and water; it is a greater and higher harmonious creation than you, a divine product, with a more wonderful life and action in its substance than you carry in your little brain, with which you contribute but an atom to its life. In vain you will dream of an after-life, if you fail to recognize the life about you.

What does the anatomist see when he examines the brain of man? A tangle of white filaments, the meaning of which he cannot decipher. And what does it see in itself? A world of light, tones, thoughts, memories, fancies, sensations of love and hate. And so realize the relation of that which you, standing outside the world, see in it, to that which it sees in itself, and do not require that both, the outer and the inner, shall appear more alike in the totality of the world than in you, who are but a part of it. And only because you are a part of this world, see in yourself also a part of that which it sees in itself.

And finally, do you perhaps still ask why our ultimate body, as we call it, only awakens in the other life after we have expelled it here in this earthly realm, and why it is already the continuation of our limited body?

That which in this narrower existence dies, is indeed destroyed; it is nothing but an instance of the same universal law which prevails through the whole of this world; a proof that it still continues into the next. Doubter, if you must always reason alone from this life—be it so.

The living strength of consciousness never really rises anew, is never lost, but, like that of the body upon which it rests, can only change its place, its form, its manner of dissemination in time and space, only sink to-day or here, to mount to-morrow or elsewhere; only rise to-day or here, to sink to-morrow or elsewhere.[1]

For the eye to be awake so that you see consciously, the ear must be hushed to sleep; to arouse the inner world of thought, the outward senses must be subdued into quiescence; a pain in the smallest spot can quite exhaust your soul's consciousness. The more the light of observation is dispersed, the more feebly is

[1] Indisputably this law, analogous to the so-called law of the conservation of energy in the physical realm, is in some way connected with it through the fundamental relation of spirit to body, without the connection being clearly established, or shown to be derivable psychophysically from the physical law, since the essence of psychophysical energy itself is not clearly defined. The law must therefore be inferred from facts such as are above mentioned; and, without being exactly and fully proved, it acquires thereby a probability which qualifies it to serve as a basis for such views as are here in question.

any single part illuminated; the more clearly it strikes one point, the more all else enters into darkness; to reflect upon some one thing means abstraction from all besides. For your present freshness you have to thank your sleep since yesterday, the more deeply you sleep to-day the more brightly you will awake to-morrow, and the more vigilantly you have passed the waking hours the more profoundly you will sleep.

But the sleep of man in this world is in reality only a half sleep, which allows the body to wake again because it is still present; not until death is the full sleep which allows a new awaking because the body is no longer there; yet the old law is still present, which demands an equivalent for the former consciousness, and hence the new body as a continuation of the old; therefore a new consciousness will also be present as an equivalent and continuation of the old.

As a continuation of the old! For that which enables the body of the old man to still bear the consciousness which the body of the child, no atom of which is longer his, bore, will enable the future body to bear the same consciousness which was in the body of the aged man, of which it no longer possesses an atom. So it is that every successor preserves within himself and is built up by the continuation of the actions of him who bore the earlier consciousness. This is therefore a law, which ordains the onward march of the life here from to-day to to-morrow, and from this life to the other. And can there be another law so fundamental as this of the eternal survival of man?

And so do not ask, how it is that effects which you produce in this outward world, which are outside you, shall still belong to you more than any others which are also outside. It is because the former much more than the latter have gone out from you. Every cause retains its effects as an eternal possession. But in truth your effects have never gone out from you; even in this world they formed the unconscious continuation of your existence, only awaiting the awakening to new consciousness.

As little as a man can ever die who has once lived, so little could he be awakened to life had he not lived before; it is only that he had not lived as an individual. The consciousness with which the child awakes at birth is only a part of the eternal, pre-existing, universal, divine consciousness which has concentrated itself in the new soul. We can indeed as little follow

79

the ways and the changes of the living force of consciousness as those of the vital energy of the body.

But are you afraid that human consciousness, because born out of the universal, will again flow back into it; then look at the tree. Many years passed before the branches came out of the trunk; but once there they do not go down into it again. How would the tree grow and develop if this happened? So too will the life tree of the world grow and unfold itself.

After all, the strong argument in this world for the other is not from reasons unknown to us, nor from suppositions which we make, but it is from facts that we do know that we base our conclusions on the greater and higher facts of the future life, thereby strengthening and confirming a faith, practically demanded, depending upon a higher point of view and to be set in living relations with life. Indeed, if we did not need this faith, wherefore strengthen it; yet how use it, if it remain unsupported.

CHAPTER TEN

THE SOUL of man permeates his whole body; when it abandons the body, forthwith the body dies; yet light of consciousness of the soul is now here, now there.[1]

We have just seen it wandering back and forth within the narrow body, lighting up in turn the eye,

[1] In scientific terms one can say: Consciousness is everywhere; it is awake when and wherever the bodily energy underlying the spiritual, the so-called psychophysical, exceeds that degree of strength which we call the threshold. (Compare p. 72, note.) According to this, consciousness can be localized in time and space. The highest point of our psychophysical activity wavers, as it were, from one place to another, wherewith the light of consciousness changes its place, only that during this life it fluctuates back and forth within our body simply, indeed, within a limited part of this body, and in sleep sinks quite below the threshold, above which, on waking, it rises again.

(Compare on this point "Elemente der Psychophysik," II. Kap. p. 40 and 41.)

the ear, the inner and the outer senses, finally, in death, to depart from it wholly, just as one, whose little house in which he has for long moved about back and forth is destroyed, goes out into the open and begins a new pilgrimage. Death makes no division between the two lives except to allow the exchange of the narrower scene of action for the wider. And as little as the light of consciousness is always and everywhere the same in this life, where it can be so interrupted and dispersed, so will it be in the future life. It is only that the field of action is unspeakably larger, the possible extension wider, the ways freer, the points of view higher, embracing all the lower ones of this world.

But even in this life exceptionally, in rare cases, we see the light of consciousness wander out of the narrower body into the wider and return again, bringing news of what happens in distant spaces, in distant time. For the length of the future depends on the breadth of the present. Suddenly a rift shows itself in the otherwise forever closed door between this life and the other, to close again quickly—the door, which will wholly open in death, and only then will open never more to be closed. But a mere glance through the rift in advance is not profitable. Yet the exception to the law of this life is only an example of the greater law of life which embraces at once the two worlds.

It may happen that the earthly body falls asleep in one direction deeply enough to allow it in others to awaken far beyond its usual limits, and yet not so deeply and completely as to awaken no more. Or, to the subjective vision there comes a flash so unusually vivid as to bring to the earthly sense an impression rising above the threshold from an otherwise inaccessible distance. Here begin the wonders of clairvoyance, of presentiments, and premonitions in dreams: pure fables, if the future body and the future life are fables; otherwise signs of the one and predictions of the other; but what has signs exists, and what has prophecies will come.

And yet there are no signs in the normal life of this world. The present has to build the heavenly body only for the future, not yet to see and hear with the eye and ear that are to be. The blossom does not thrive that is prematurely broken off. And even if one can assist his faith in the future life by belief in these traces of its shining into the present life, yet one should not build upon it. Healthy faith is based upon fundamentals and limits itself to the highest point of view of normal life, of which it forms a part.

You have hitherto believed that the light form in which a dead person appears to you in remembrance is merely your own interior illusion. You are mistaken; it is itself a reality, which, with conscious step, not only comes to you but enters into you. The earlier form is still its spiritual raiment; only, no longer fettered with its former dense body and wandering inactive in its company, but transparent, light, divested of its earthly burden, for the moment it is now here, now there, following the voice of each one who calls to the dead, or of itself appearing to you, to suggest the thought of the dead. Indeed the common conception of the appearance of souls in the future life has always been of light, immaterial forms, independent of the limits of space, and so, though unintentionally, the truth has been reached.

You have also heard ghosts spoken of. Doctors call them phantasms, hallucinations. So they are for the living, yet, at the same time, they are actual apparitions of the dead, as we call them. For though they be the weaker forms of memory in us, how should they not also be the more pronounced corresponding appa-

84

ritions. Therefore, why still dispute whether they are the one or the other when they are at once both. And why be afraid of ghosts, when you do not fear the remembered forms within you which they already are.

And yet the reason for this is not wanting. Unlike the forms you have yourself summoned or which of themselves steal gently and peacefully into the fabric of your inner life, mingling helpfully with it, they advance, and surprise you, with overpowering force, apparently coming before you, really entering into you and bringing into your mind far more dismay than comfort. To live at once in the two worlds makes a morbid existence. The dead and the living should not communicate. To approach the dead so nearly as to see them as clearly and objectively as they are able to see each other means for the living already a partial death; hence the terror of the living before such apparitions of the dead; it is also a partial backsliding of the dead away from the realm beyond death into that this side of it; from this comes the saying—and perhaps more than saying—that only those spirits wander about which are not quite released, which still by heavy fetters are earth-bound. To drive away the unblest, call for the help of a better and stronger spirit;

but the best and the strongest is the Spirit of all spirits. Who can harm you under His protection? And so is verified the saying that before the voice of God every evil spirit vanishes.

Meanwhile in this sphere of spiritual sickness faith itself is threatened with the contagion of superstition. The simplest way to guard oneself against the coming of ghosts is not to believe in their coming; for to believe that they come is to meet them halfway.

As they are able to appear to each other, I said. For the same apparition which is against the order of this world is but taken prematurely from the order of the other. The dwellers in the other world will appear to each other in a luminous, clear, full, and objective form, of which we in our memory of them have but a weak echo, a dim outline drawing, because they pervade each other with their full and complete being, only a little part of which reaches each of us through memory of them. Only there as well as here attention needs to be focussed upon the appearance in order to behold it.

Now, it may still be asked: how is it possible that they so unite and appear so objectively and definitely to each other? But ask first, how is it possible that what is received by you as the semblance of a living person, and what is conveyed to your brain by the memory of a dead one—and there is nothing else before you to base it upon—appears in the one case as an objective perception, but in the other as a circumscribed memory? The no longer exact impression which underlies the mental picture deludes you as to the outline of the form from which it proceeded in the beginning. You cannot know why from the plane of this world; how can you expect to know from that of the other?

And so I repeat: do not conclude from arguments of this world which you do not know, nor from suppositions which you make, but from facts clear to you here as to the greater and higher facts of the life to come. Any single conclusion may be erroneous; even that one which we have just reached; therefore, do not be satisfied with any isolated proof: the final conviction in regard to them, which we have to demand before and beyond every conclusion, will be the best support of our faith below, and our best guide on the upward path.

But once lay hold upon faith directly from above, and the whole path of belief which will lead us upwards opens easily before us here.

CHAPTER ELEVEN

Y ET HOW EASY all would be for faith if man could but accustom himself to see more than a mere word in the saying with which he has played for more than a thousand years, that in God he lives and moves and has his being. Then were faith in God one with his own eternal life, he would see his own eternal life as belonging to that of God himself, and in the advancement of his future above his present stage of life would perceive only a loftier structure above a lower one in God, such as he already has latent within him; he would comprehend the greater from the lesser model, and in the union of both the whole, of which he is but a part.

Perception in you dissolves, and memory ascends from it within you; your whole life of intuition dissolves in God, and a higher existence of recollection rises from it to God; and like memories in your mind, so the spirits of the other world communicate within in the divine mind. It is only one step above another on the same ladder which leads, not to God, but upwards within Him, who in Himself is at once the base and the summit. With that saying void of thought, how empty God was; in its full significance, how rich He is!

Do you, then, know how the further spiritual life of perception is possible? You know only that it is real; but it is only possible to a soul. You can therefore, although ignorant how it is possible, easily believe in the reality of a future for your whole soul within a higher one; you must only believe that there is a higher soul, and that you are it.

And again, how easy it would all be for faith, if man could habitually see a truth in that further word, that God lives and moves and has His being in all. Then it were not a dead, but, through God, a living world, out of which man is building his future body and is thereby creating a new abode within the dwelling place of God.

But when will this vitalizing faith become a living one?

He who makes it living will himself be made alive.

CHAPTER TWELVE

YOU ASK as to the whether. I answer with the how. Faith does without the question whether; but if asked, the one answer is through the how; and so long as the how does not stand fast, the whether will not cease from troubling.

Here stands the tree; many a single leaf may fall from it; yet its root and its unity are firm and perfect. It will always develop new branches, and new leaves will continue to fall; the tree itself will not fall: it will put forth blossoms of beauty, and instead of being rooted in faith, it will bear the fruits of faith.

THE
BEYOND

THE FUTURE LIFE OF MEMORY

THE CONCRETE tangibility of our present life may indeed vanish later on, our hands may one day be unable to grasp our bodies, we may be unable to drag our weary steps along, unable to move and carry burdens as we did here below. All that will lie behind us, in the grave, and, in all these respects, our future life may readily be more lacking in power and strength than our present one. For indisputably, the relation of sensory debilitation that exists between concept and memory will also be reflected between our conceptual and memory lives in the higher regions of the spirit. The analogy will suffer no rift, and thus our future memory life may appear in general to be light, transparent and airy, externally intangible, as opposed to our present heavy, thick, satiated form of life which is grasped with the coarser senses, and can only be grasped with these senses. Instead of heavy, manifest body forms it is possible that light, more freely mobile figures of memory may pass through the mind of the higher spirit; we shall discuss this later. The question now is not only to meditate upon this physical debilitation of our future memory life as opposed to our present conceptual life, but also upon the intensification of our future memory life as opposed to the present one, an intensification which is connected with that very debilitation.

Indeed, it is the same circumstances which, in death, permit our present conceptual life to become pale, weak and colorless that, henceforth, will make our erstwhile pale, weak, colorless, indistinct memory life grow light, strong, vivid, colorful, full, determined; in other words, bring about the transmutation of our conceptual life here below into the memory life of the world beyond. The conceptual life does not perish in death; rather does it ascend and aspire to a higher life, just as the life of the caterpillar and the chrysalis does not perish when the butterfly emerges, but, along with the butterfly itself, rises to a higher, freer, lighter form. Of course, it no longer exists as a form of caterpillar or chrysalis life, and it may be said that here direct considerations touch the analogical.

Let us see. Even now, the more thoroughly all my

94

senses are closed to external things, the more I withdraw into the gloaming of the outer world, the more aware and bright will be my memory life, and things long forgotten will come back to me. Death, on the other hand, does nothing but extinguish the senses entirely and for all time, so that all possibility of reviving them is also extinguished. No closing of the eye during our lifetime can be so profound, no awakening of memories so luminous as in death. What the closing of the eye during life does only temporarily, superficially, for a brief day and for only one sense, the long, last closing of the eye does for the sum of our senses, having reference to the entire body, to the whole of life, to a higher spirit and a higher body, whereas the closing of the eye during life had only affected the image in the eye. All the force which is divided between our conceptual and our memory lives in this world becomes, in the next, the property of our memory life only, and our present memory life owes its weakness to the very fact that our conceptual life here below claims the greater part of the strength that is bestowed upon us by the higher spirit. Complete remembrance of the former life will begin only when that life lies entirely behind us, and all remembrance during that lifetime is but a brief preview of what lies ahead.

What we experience now in memory and the higher things related thereto is, as it were, but a gentle breath that rises above our present conceptual life, as a soft vapor floats invisibly above its watery source, leading the way to the same blue sky to which, finally, the entire body of water aspires. But if we try to destroy or do away with the water, if we scatter it to the four winds, since we cannot really destroy or do away with it any more than we can a human being— although there is apparent success in both cases—in a word, if it all changes into steam, how much broader, more powerful will be the effects generated by this steam, to make which the entire body of water has risen invisibly, than that which rose only as a pre-figuration from its surface. Indeed, how much broader, more diverse, more imperceptible in detail and, on the whole, more powerful are its effects than those of the very water which underwent the change! In the clouds, at sun-up and at sunset, in rain, in thunder and in lightning, it can now play a most important rôle in nature's household, due to its new, higher, freer, brighter, lighter, clearer state. Meanwhile, we are probably of the foolish opinion that it is done with, just because we can no longer take it with our hands or pour it into a certain glass.

RELATION OF THE
SPIRITUAL TO THE PHYSICAL

T O BE SURE, it may appear to the superficial observer that the influences and works which emanate from us to the outside world soon become indifferently scattered and lose contact both with each other and with ourselves, in consequence of which there can be no question of unification or unity. But to the deeper, inquiring mind it appears quite otherwise. To the extent that man himself is united, the circle of his acts and works is also united in itself, and he remains united with it. Thus, in reality, he appears to himself to be but the continued growth, the further expansion of his narrow bodily system.

Let us watch a swan making furrows on a pond. However far it may swim, its tracks still keep together; not only the original tracks, but all the ripples we see spreading out from these tracks, for each point of the track sends forth a ripple and all of them keep together, as do the tracks themselves. They even run over into each other, and the further they spread the deeper and more inextricable the connection becomes.

Quite as unified as the tracks of the swan in the water, however, is the life course of man, and equally unified and intertwined are all the influences that emanate from him during his life's course. Whether he travel over land or sea, the beginning of his course remains linked to its end, as do all the influences that emanate from it. Nor is it otherwise as he travels from youth to the grave.

Of course, the swan can fly up out of the water and alight again at another point. Then there do seem to be two separate wave tracks, which is indeed true, in the water. In the air, however, they remain connected through a system of waves. Actually, man is as little able as is the swan to break away from his connection with earth, water, air and whatever else of an imponderable nature enters into the earthly constitution. So wherever he may go, run or leap, whatever his standing or condition, whatever he may say, write or touch, the system of acts and works, of movements and institutions that emerges from the totality of all this, can never come to grief. During the course of life, it can only continue to expand or

99

to enrich with greater diversity movements in which earlier movements continue to foregather with later ones, thus bringing about new modifications of existing institutions in the same way that they take place in our restricted bodies. Each new movement that emanates from man to the outer world, each work in the creation of which he expends his force and activity, makes a new contribution, so to speak, to the evolution of his future body, which is still partly attached to the earlier, expanding works, still predestinedly clings to them. If we could survey with one all-embracing glance all the movements and institutions, briefly, all the acts and works which have gone forth from a man during his entire life-time, not only would we find them involved and entangled among themselves, in the same way that the matter, motions and institutions of our body are involved and entangled, but the very matter to which these motions have been transmitted, and which is the bearer of these institutions, would also assume the form of a perfect continuum, just as the matter of our present body has done, without having, for this reason, any specified frontier other than the matter composing the earthly domain.

However, the same inter-dependence which may be traced through the spatial sphere may also be traced through the temporal. Perhaps we do not believe it at first, but it is certain that all the influences which have emanated from Christ to the world, and which have been transmitted to his confessors and through his confessors, have come down to us not only because of a perfectly continuous chain of material sequences, but also because these material sequences still form a perfectly continuous and connected system, and that they are, so to speak, nothing other than the far-off and, at the same time, interdependent wave expansions of the track the swan left during its lifetime.

What Christ taught through word and example had an effect on His disciples through sound and light; it brought out something different in them, drove them to new deeds. Through the word, through example and action, the effect was transmitted further, not only to men but also beyond men, and, as the fruit of actual experience, its influence even went forth into the outer world. There developed in Church, state, art and science, in the entire life of Christians everywhere, new institutions, new ways of approaching things, of meditating upon them, of handling them generally; and all the institutions and conditions prevailing throughout the whole of Christendom remain necessarily linked together through the services of intermediaries who are never lacking wherever Christians are to be found. As it happens, Christ's actions followed one another in close succession during his lifetime, and it is now impossible that anything dependent on this fact, even the farthest removed, most divergent consequences, should lose contact with other equally dependent factors; just as the leaves and blossoms of branches that are farthest from the root and themselves most divergent, nevertheless remain connected with one another. And let us note that this is not the purely external connection that results from propinquity. It is a connection based on action, on mutual influence and contact of one with the other; a working connection, such as is now also required of us, as the conveyors of a spiritual action. If the spiritual results of Christ's teaching, which are transmitted through material elements, had remained at times unconnected and inactive, how would it be possible to speak of a Christian community, of a Christian church? Not being ourselves the spirit of

Christ, but members of his community, we only receive His influence, which sends its branches into us, and therefore, we cannot possess the self-conviction with which Christ Himself, in His community, continues to live, to conserve and develop His own spirit.

Now, that which emerges in the case of Christ as a distinct, grandiose phenomenon applies as well to the least distinguished of men. It is not the manner of continued duration, but the significance of that which endures and the value of relationship to the higher spirit, that is different. No man's life is without consequences that remain always and eternally. Everything in the world that was changed because he was there, and would not be so if he had not been there, is a part of these consequences, and their whole wide circle remains, for each human being, quite as closely linked together as was the narrow circle of life at the beginning.

THE LIVING BODY
CREATES THE PRECONDITIONS
FOR THE FUTURE LIFE

I T IS CURIOUS that, as regards the question of immortality, we should generally be concerned only with what follows the destruction of the body in death, and since we can see only horror and decay, we are perplexed as to the future physical vehicle of the soul. In order to again possess a living body, we must consider not only the emanations of the body in death, and ensuingly of the corpse, but also those of the living body during our entire life-time, not only from the standpoint of matter but also of the effects produced. In other words, we must consider in its entirety the complete inter-relationship of all these emanations. For it is the living body that creates during and by means of our entire present life the physical pre-conditions of our entire future life. In the end, this confining body of ours will decay and nothing further need emanate from it after death. Already, while alive, it has done its part towards that which is to come later, and the ultimate function it fulfills is that of passing away, this being, in itself, a condition of the awakening of man to the new body and the new life. The fact that in the old body and the old life consciousness no longer has reason to exist is, itself, the explanation of the fact that man awakens to the consciousness of a new body and a new life in which all former matter, movement and force are regained. It is for this reason that matter, movement and force drive so restlessly through our bodies while we are in this world, that life stirs so indefatigably in us, and so long as life lasts we should try to endure these things in order that, in the other world, our bodies and our lives may become rich and great and mighty. Our little body here below is but a tiny loom through which pass all the threads of the broad fabric that is being spun to make the body and life of the world to come. This broad fabric itself, however, is nothing but a new one spun into the great Weaver's organization, of which the tiny, living loom is also but a part. For in this domain everything takes place in the inner, not in the outer world. For the most part, we are inclined to believe that death first restores the body to nature, after which it becomes disintegrated, is lost, passes away, and we are afraid that our souls too may pass away with it. Why do we not rather fear life, in which this is an infinitely more frequent occurrence than in death? For life is a process of disintegration which is constantly throwing us back into nature. Death, on the other hand, is not the entrance into, but rather the end of this process of disintegration, an end, however, following which the matter involved passes on into the building of a new, greater structure, and, in fact, the same forces which disappear in the present structure serve to create the new one. Indeed, it is not only the matter coursing through our bodies that is involved. This is rather the life substance, the ferment, the leaven dough from which our forces will gain a vantage point that will permit them to seize upon the whole body of the earth and claim it as peculiarly their own.

In his book entitled "Physis," Carus wrote: "We must not think that the processes of destruction and disintegration of life occur, perhaps, only in the degree to which we perceive them in the corpse, whose atoms are only very gradually surrendered to the general life of nature. No! this process of disintegration of life takes place much more quickly than that of death, inasmuch, for instance, as we can calculate that out of the entire mass of blood which passes through the veins in the course of a day, about a fourth part of it is disintegrated and eliminated in various ways."

Much more important, however, than the industry and speed with which man imposes the matter of his body upon the outer world, and keeps on creating from it only that he may impose it again, is the entirely related industry with which he pursues his activities. Consumption of substance and consumption of force go together. And what masses of living force are transformed during a man's lifetime into actions directed to the outer world! Indeed, the influences which emanate from man to the outer world, as we shall show later in greater detail, pass through the whole earth, whereas only a limited quantity of matter can pass through his body directly to the outer world.

We might ask, what happens to the infant who dies immediately after birth, before he has had time to exert an influence from within or about himself? Will he be lost? Even though he has lived only a moment, he must live eternally. For the substance, motion and strength to which his life and consciousness were attached can never again vanish from the world, but must be present again in the world after his death, in the form of some further-reaching influence, which may not even be carried on by ourselves. Needless to say, there is no question of such a complex system as is involved when an adult dies. But just as the child here below could have developed further from feeble beginnings, so will it be in the other world. In that world, however, he will begin life as the same child he was when he died.

ANALOGY OF MAN
WITH PLANT AND ANIMAL

ALL PLANTS first develop quietly in the seed and then, with the bursting and destruction of the pod, they awaken into a new domain of air and light. In the same manner, all animals first develop quietly in the egg, whether inside a womb, like ourselves, or outside, and through the bursting and destruction of their shells, they enter into this same domain, along with the rest of us and with the entire plant world. Indeed, we can already see, in the case of many living creatures, the formation of one stratum on top of the other which, from time immemorial, has served as a basis for envisaging a future life. After the plant has stepped forth into air and light, a wholly new life opens to it once again, when, later, it spreads out its blossom to the enjoyment of light. Thus, too, the butterfly, after having passed through the egg, caterpillar and chrysalis stages, breaks through the husk of the chrysalis and acquires wings for the sluggish caterpillar feet, a thousand eyes for his dull face. It may be noted that even the embryonic period and even, so far as we know, that still earlier period, which exists in all animals as well as in man, that might be called an earlier life—preceding the formation of the egg itself and the transition from the state of infertility into that of fertility, after which new development begins—is also characterized by the destruction of that which, in the first period, had appeared to be the principal, the most important kernel, the very nucleus of everything; to wit, through destruction of the germ-cell. This forms the greater part of the egg, according to the stage of embryonic growth, but it is destroyed (we do not yet know how, or whether simultaneously with or shortly after the exit) when the egg leaves the ovary to develop into the embryo.

Many things we have already noted in connection with man, we now see applied in a more general way.

For instance: the same material world in which the seed is engendered and then sheltered is also that into which the plant shoots up and takes root. In the same material world in which an egg lies in a nest and a caterpillar creeps on the ground, a bird and a butterfly are flying about. In the same material world which contains the human foetus there also lives man already born; the mother's womb is, after all, only a part, a narrower district of that world. The seed is not planted here in the earth, that the plant may send forth its shoots on another planet, nor is the egg laid here that the bird, after the shell is burst, may find itself somewhere beyond the Milky Way. On the contrary, seed and plant, egg and bird, human embryo and man live beside, between, indeed, in one another. The later evolutionary stratum still enjoys the same world space everywhere that the earlier one did. The higher evolutionary stratum recognizes this as true, but the lower one does not recognize it.

Thus, we should not entertain the idea that, through our death, we are to be projected into quite another world. On the contrary, we shall continue to live in the same world in which we now live, only we shall have other, new means of comprehending it, and greater liberty to traverse it. It will be the same old world in which later we shall fly and in which we now creep. Why make a new garden when, in the old garden, flowers bloom for which, in the new life, a new vision and new organs of enjoyment are evolving? The same earthly plants serve caterpillars and butterflies, but how different they appear to the butterfly than to the caterpillar, and whereas the caterpillar clings to one plant, the butterfly flies through the whole garden.

We now see nothing around us of the beings who have preceded us into the future existence, or else we believe we see nothing of their existence. But let us ask ourselves if the caterpillar knows anything of the life of the butterfly, if the chicken beneath the dome of the egg knows anything of the life of the bird under the celestial dome, or if the human foetus, in the mother's narrow womb knows anything about the life of man in the great world organism. The butterfly flies past the caterpillar, touches it slightly in passing, and to the caterpillar it seems a foreign body. The caterpillar would have to have the eyes of the butterfly itself in order to regard it as one of its own. Inside the egg, on the chicken's head, the eyes are already pre-formed, but the chicken does not yet know their use. It would have to open them first and get rid of the enclosing shell in order to see the bird high up under the same celestial roof as itself. Will things be different in our own case? May we not also expect that with the bursting of the shell of our present bodies there will open up means of perception, which our present life has already pre-formed in us, that will permit us to see for the first time those who were born before us into the new life and who, even now, might be living and operating between and around us, indeed, in us even.

After the bursting of the pod the seed becomes a similar plant to the one which bore it, the egg becomes a similar bird to the one which carried the egg in itself, the human foetus will one day become a similar man to him who carried in himself the egg of man, or the foetus. What is it then that, according to this analogy, carries man like an egg inside itself? It is the whole of earthly nature surrounding him; and thus we may expect that after our own awakening, our spirits will also find bodies similar to surrounding nature, bodies which they will consciously master and move with animation. One day we shall be similar to the nature that now surrounds us.

To be sure, another nature for each man, after the bursting of his bonds, will not be realized on the plane of matter; from the standpoint of matter and spatial volume there will never be but one nature, but this one nature will be different for each man, according to the mastery, understanding and stimulation which, under different conditions and in different forms, he has to offer. His future manner as regards this, however, will be preconditioned by the manner in which he now comes in contact with nature.

Of course, the flower withers at last, and the butterfly dies in the end. Shall we, too, after our future life, finally wither and die?

But suppose we reverse the speculation. Should not this decay and dying be as apparent for the souls of plants and animals as ours is for us?

Does not ordinary faith already permit us to walk one day in a garden of Paradise? But whence come the flowers, butterflies and birds into that garden? I imagine they come from the same place that men have come into the garden. Not only is man raised in death to a higher domain, but along with him the whole interdependent chain of living beings, in accordance with a plan which, in itself, is interdependent.

It seems to me, indeed, very awkward for the faith in immortality to make an exception of the immortality of man, or even, as is done by many people, to relate it to the especially higher virtues of man so that only the intellectually or morally gifted would participate in immortality. Here the most primitive peoples seem to me to have found the best answer. The inhabitant of Lappland thinks he will find his reindeer, the Samojede his dogs, in the other life, and who among us who has a faithful dog would not also like to find it again one day? Is it really possible that there will be no creatures of a lower species than man in that other life? If the answer is yes, it is only natural that these creatures whom man meets there should grow out of those whom he has met here below.

CONTINUED
EXISTENCE OF IDEAS

GOD IS A SPIRIT. Just what a spirit is we can learn from our selves; but He is an infinite and infinitely high spirit. Now, in our spirit and in the domain of our spirits, there are narrower and wider expanses, stratifications of elevation. Let us amplify and expand till we can go no farther, in order that God may always remain a spirit like our own, in everything that makes a spirit a spirit, and in order that He may climb aloft, infinitely high and wide, above everything upon which the finiteness and the lowness, the stupidity and the narrowness of our spirits depend. To be sure, we shall not, through this, attain to an unchangeable, timeless God raised above all space; but to One who comprises all change, all time and all space in the same sense as our spirit comprises change, time and space, as being forms of His thinking, His knowledge, His entire possession of things. What we have in these forms of things, these are the things to us. What God has in these forms of things, these are the real things; and what we possess of them through Him partakes of the being and essence of things.

As a spirit, God is related to the physical world. The relation of the spiritual to the physical we learn from our selves. But God, as the most universal, the greatest, highest spirit is related to the most universal, the greatest and the highest in the physical world. We can also learn from our selves to what extent, with the expansion of the sphere, with the heightening of the scale of the spirit, the relation of the spirit to the physical is enlarged and intensified; the higher spirit is borne by an organism that is more highly developed and that carries it, so to speak, higher aloft. If we amplify and expand further in this direction, we shall find that the broadest and highest spirit is borne by the broadest and most highly developed organism, that is to say, by the world itself; not the unorganic world but the entire world, with the origins and all the histories, all the destinies of the different peoples.

God, as spirit, is also related to other spirits. To nearby spirits? That would mean that we had wrongly ascended. For the truly unique and unified God not only tolerates no other God, He tolerates no spirit near Him, each spirit being, in itself, a smaller God. Let us look more deeply into ourselves, and from the lesser God elucidate the great God. My eye sees nothing of that which my ear hears, my ear hears nothing of that which my eye sees, each one of these organs is sensorially a being isolated from the other. But both of them together are revealed to my spirit as a whole; my spirit immediately knows everything that the eye, the ear and all my other senses know individually, and it takes in still higher things of general relevance. If we amplify and expand further in this direction we find that each living creature is a being shut off from the others in feeling as well as in thought and desire; yet all of them together will be revealed to the whole spirit which will know simultaneously everything that they know separately, and will comprehend as well things of an infinitely higher nature that are still further above them.

Or do we not yet believe in God? Have the two other principles denied us their strength? Be that as it may, as the third one, it might serve towards the support and completion of that strength. That which permits us to believe in the soul of our fellow-men and in the soul of worms as well, can also permit us to believe in the right expansion and elevation of the collective soul, the emanations and parts of which we all are.

But when God's height is set above the world, instead of in an intensification of height which, from the empirical viewpoint, we can already attribute to our own spirit, since it lies above matter and the lower spheres of the senses—were this not true, in fact, the very word 'height' would become meaningless sound —when, then, it is set above the world through an elevation of God to which no empirical viewpoint may still be applied, then the principle is abandoned and, at the same time, the bridge connecting it with imagination and deduction is destroyed, thus reducing all talk of God to incomprehensible babble.

Man changes partially from day to day and, in the course of the years, he changes wholly, his body is returned to the outer world and from it a new one is created. The soul is not only a connecting principle but also the changing substance and form of the body, so that the swifter the physical change takes place the more lively is the soul. In the transformation of the body man rises gradually from one rung on the ladder of life to the next, the body expands and develops and, with the body, the soul.

If we amplify and advance further along these lines, there opens up to us the prospect that death, instead of being a gradual, partial change, is nothing other than a more rapid, more sudden transformation of the body that thus constitutes the rapid ascension to a new degree of life.

Not only is the soul already attached to but one point of the physical world, but it is the conscious principle and conveyor of a sphere of physical activities that rise and fall, expand and contract, are free to move hither and thither. During sleep they sink below the threshold above which consciousness gleams, and during waking hours they rise above it again. Now they stand still, at the zenith, and here man becomes all eye, while there he is all ear. Now they are sharpened as though to a point, so that the entire soul is directed towards one point. Now they branch out, and we are dispersed. Now they withdraw entirely into the inner world and the soul is sunk into itself; now they turn again towards the outer world, and the soul once more becomes aware of the outer world. Thus the soul follows each change of the activities it serves to unite, or shall we reverse this statement and say that the activities follow each change of the soul. As a matter of fact, neither of them follows the other but each one accompanies the other, and whenever or wherever the summit of these activities is to be found, there the life of the soul also seeks its summit, which makes it possible for us to designate the seat of the soul.

If we amplify and expand further in this direction, there opens up to us the prospect that if, already, here below, the soul moves thus in a small part of the great whole, then, in death, it will simply pass into a greater part of that whole and move, henceforth, with greater freedom.

We can destroy every part of the body, even the brain. If it is not too much at one time, the soul does not die; it does not even suffer, if the rest of the body retains its means of defense. Destruction of that which is already damaged is even the best way to destroy the damage when the means of defense are in force. If we amplify and expand further in this direction there opens up to us the prospect that even when our entire body is subject to destruction, our soul will not die, nor suffer, even, since the greater body of which our body is a part, even as our soul is a part of the soul of this body, will also have means of defense for its preservation, and that this will be the last means, in the nature of things to be foreseen, of destroying all the damage of old-age and sickness.

Let us consider an image in the eye. The body gives it substance, sap and strength, while the soul gives it sensation. Once the image is extinguished, the substance, sap and strength vanish again into the body from which they had been assembled. But for sensation there enters the memory of sensation; it enters into a new, higher domain from which float concepts and thoughts. There it encounters the remembrance of all other, earlier images and together they weave the higher life itself. If we amplify and expand further in this direction, there opens up the prospect that also when our entire image of the body shall be extinguished and its substance, sap and strength vanish again into the great body which first brought them forth, a memory echo of this life will enter into the life of the spirit that gave soul to our body and together, with the echoes of all other long departed men, that is to say, with their souls in the beyond, it will help to weave the higher life of that spirit. And, as the memory echo clings to a produced echo, which the physical image has left in us after the disappearance, so the memory echo of our life clings to a produced image, left behind in the world by our physical life.

Now, whoever wants to ponder over precisely where in the world, in the body of the great spirit, the new seat of the soul is to be found, and how it is made, may he first of all ponder—and pondering over this point he will, of course, not ponder over the other—where, in the body of the small spirit, the part of the great one, the seat of memory, is to be found and how it is made. Though it may still be long before we find an answer to either point or the other, it is no longer a question of the If, but only of the Where and the How. And also for the Where and the How there are to be found in our principle sufficient reference points of representation and conclusion.

Before birth, the child is enclosed inside the womb. With the bursting of all former bonds—it would appear to be his death—he steps outside into a quite new, free empire that is not detached from the former one, but rather encloses it, and he has free intercourse with all those who have stood on the same rung of life's ladder. If we amplify and expand further in this direction, there opens up to us the prospect that with the breaking of the present bonds of life—again, apparently, our death—we step into a still more free, quite new domain, which is yet not detached from the other, but rather encloses it in a wider circle, and we mingle still more freely with those who have stood on the same rung of life's ladder.

And thus we may proceed from the most diverse points of view; nothing is needed save expansion and amplification along the lines of our principle. So we find ourselves led from this side to the beyond, not in contradiction, but on the basis of the facts of the world below.

EDITORIAL NOTE

The sections assembled under the heading "The Beyond" are taken from later works by G. Th. Fechner and are published for the first time in English translation.

The Future Life of Memory from: *Zend Avesta*, III, p.14-17

Relation of the Spiritual to the Physical from: *Zend Avesta*, III, p. 118-123

The Living Body Creates the Preconditions for the Future Life from: *Zend Avesta*, III, p. 128-131

Analogy of Man with Plant and Animal from: *Zend Avesta*, III, p. 229-234

Continued Existence of Ideas from: *Ueber die Seelenfrage*, p. 117-123